MAGURK

A DOG'S LIFE

BY RICHARD BREEN & LYN STONE

Published in Great Britain in 1999
by Penny Publishing Limited

Written by Richard Breen. Illustrated by Lyn Stone.
Compilation copyright © 1999 Penny Publishing Limited. Text copyright © 1999 Richard Breen.
Illustration copyright © 1999 Lyn Stone. Designer Tom Gordon

All rights reserved. No part of this publication may be reproduced, stored in a retrieval system, transmitted in any form or by any means, electronic, mechanical, photocopying, recording or otherwise, without the prior written permission of the copyright owner.

Contents

At Home
In Town
On Holiday

...lifetime guarantee... treated to withstand the

toughest stains...

"I do love a challenge."

MACORK

MACORK

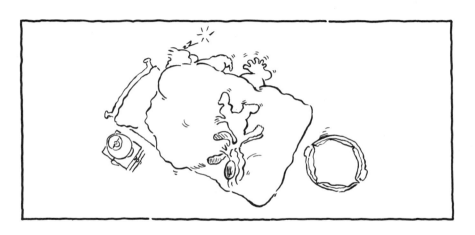

"Ahhh! My own waterbed"

MACORK

"I always gets the blame."

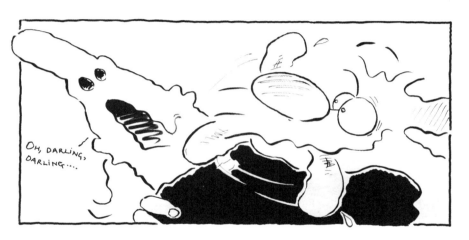

"But this always works."

MACORK

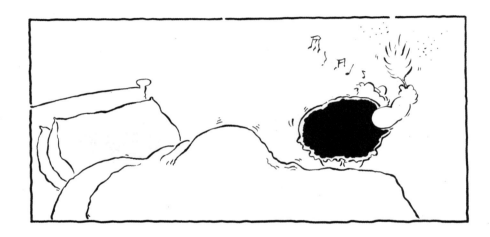

"What's the problem. When I first arrived you said Mi casa es tu casa."

"How did she know?"

AT HOME

"Humans have no idea how to sing..."

AT HOME

"Wooooooo!!"

"Peace and quiet"

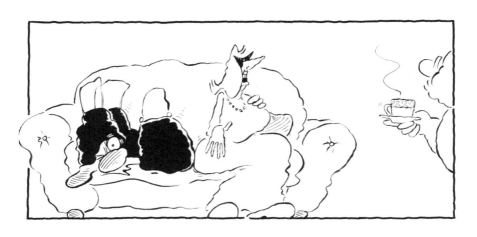

"I hate that woman."

MACORK

MACORK

"Her senile dementia has its good points."

MACORK

"Now look who's laughing."

MACORK

"Rise and sh-hine"

MACORK

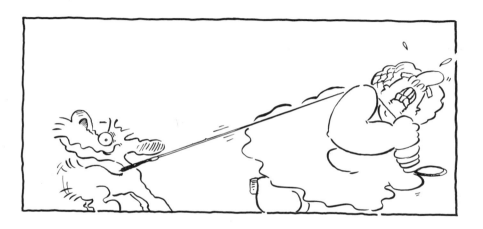

"She likes to play like this all day."

"Pathetic."

"THAT'S exercise!"

"Ooh, I feel so sick..."

"It must have been the mutton vindaloo and prune juice."

MACORK

"Run faster or we'll never catch them..."

MACORK

"It's all in the wrist."

MACORK

"I'd better slow down, or she'll never catch me."

MACORK

"*Wrong species anyway.*"

MACORK

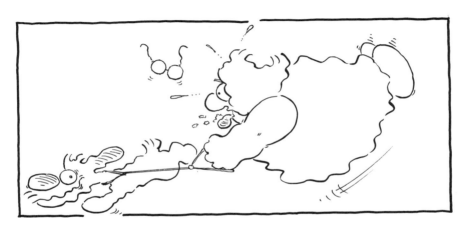

"I have to exercise her three times a day!"

MACORK

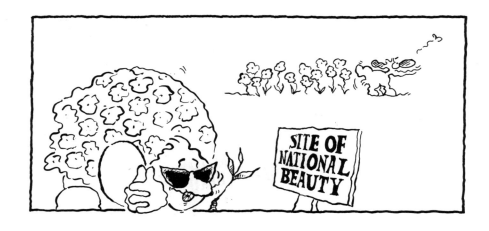

IN TOWN

MACORK

"And that's just her pack lunch!"

Macork, you look so ridiculous!

ON HOLIDAY

"She's got a nerve..."

"There is the doggie paddle..."

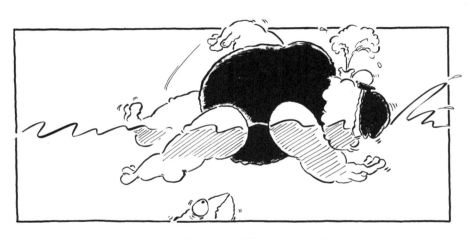

"...and the paddle steamer!"

MACORK

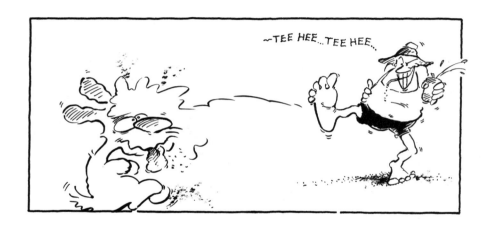

ON HOLIDAY

"Tee hee! Tee hee! Tee hee!"

MACORK

"THIS is walkies ?!"

"Vicious killer, King of the jungle... that's me!"

"Maybe not!"

"It didn't work for King Canute either..."

MACORK

ON HOLIDAY

"*Peace man, peace.*"

MACORK

ON HOLIDAY

"*That's MY exercise done.*"

"Go on, sock it to me..."

"Oops! Good game, good game"

MACORK

"WATER !"   *"WATER !"*

ON HOLIDAY

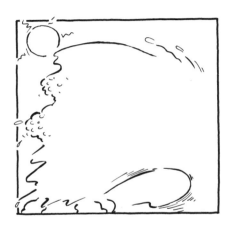

"Beautiful, what do you mean?"

"I can't see a single lamppost"

MACORK

"Sniff, that's Pinky..."

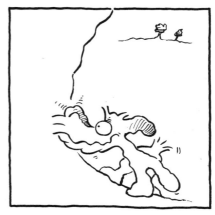

"Sniff, that's Butch"

ON HOLIDAY

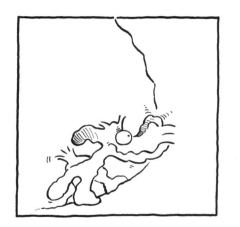 

"Well, hellooo! Who's THAT?!!"

MACORK

"Ggrrrrh!"

ON HOLIDAY

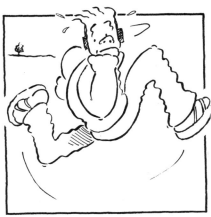

"Now THIS is jogging"

*Visit Macork at www.pennypublishing.com
for daily cartoon strips!!*

Also published by Penny Publishing Ltd

Funny Insults
Funny Money
Funny Endings
Funny Countries
Oxford Oddfellows & Funny Tales
Cambridge Oddfellows & Funny Tales
Kings & Queens -The Good, The Bad & The Ugly!